The Case of the Secret Code

Written by
Glen Robinson

Book 2
created by
Jerry D. Thomas

Pacific Press® Publishing Association
Nampa, Idaho
Oshawa, Ontario, Canada

Edited by Jerry D. Thomas
Designed by Dennis Ferree
Cover art by Stephanie Britt
Illustrations by Mark Ford
Typeset in Jansen Text 14/17

Library of Congress Cataloging-in-Publication Data:

Robinson, Glen, 1953-
     The case of the secret code / written by Glen Robinson.
         p.   cm. — (The shoebox kids ; 2)
     Summary: When Willie, confined to a wheelchair, receives coded
messages signed "G.O.D." on his computer, he needs the help of
other Shoebox Kids, as well as prayer, to identify the writer and
find Willie's missing dog.
     ISBN 0-8163-1249-4
     [1. Ciphers. 2. Computers. 3. Christian life. 4. Physically
handicapped. 5. Mystery and dectective stories.]   I. Title.
II. Series.
PZ7.R56615Cas   1995
dc20   94-23914
                                                          CIP
                                                          AC

04 05 • 5 4 3

Contents

Hi!

The Shoebox Kids are back! Many kids who read about them in *Primary Treasure* wrote and asked for more stories. So we decided to give the Shoebox Kids their own books!

The Shoebox Kids Series will have Maria and Chris and DeeDee and Willie and Jenny and Sammy tied up in new adventures and mysteries.

In *The Case of the Secret Code*, Willie starts getting strange messages on his computer. Could they really be from God?

The Case of the Secret Code is written by a good friend, Glen Robinson. He's created a story that talks about more than just computers and codes. While Willie and Chris and Maria look for clues about the mysterious messages and Willie's missing dog, they all learn something important about prayer.

As always, reading about the Shoebox Kids is more than just fun—it's about learning what the Bible really means—at home, at school, or on the playground. If you're trying to be a friend of Jesus', then the Shoebox Kids books are just for you!

Can you figure out the secret codes before Willie does? Have fun trying!

Jerry D. Thomas

P.S. Another Shoebox Kids book is coming soon!

CHAPTER 1

The Secret Message

Willie Teller stared at his computer screen and couldn't believe it. He rubbed his eyes, but the numbers wouldn't go away. Who on earth would send him a message in secret code?

It all started when his parents went on an out-of-town trip together. Grandpa came to stay with Willie and brought some good news. He had ordered a modem for Willie's computer.

"What's a modem, Grandpa?" Willie asked.

"It's a machine that lets your computer talk to other computers over the telephone."

It had seemed funny, computers talking to

each other. *I wonder if they tell each other jokes*, Willie thought as he sat on the front porch, sharing a bowl of ice cream with Coco.

Ruff! Coco begged for another bite.

"OK, one more." As he dropped a spoonful into Coco's bowl, the mail carrier walked up the sidewalk, carrying a brown package.

"Here you go, Willie," the mail carrier said. "This package is for you."

"Thanks, Mr. Davis." Just then, Grandpa came out to say Hi.

"Hey, Grandpa," Willie said as Mr. Davis listened, "I've got a joke for you. What did the computer say after he was finished cutting the lawn?"

The mail carrier looked at Willie, puzzled. "I didn't know computers could do that." He looked at Grandpa and winked.

"It's a riddle, Mr. Davis. Come on!" Willie grinned.

"I give up, Willie," Grandpa said. "What did the computer say after he was finished cutting the lawn?"

"Modem. Get it? *Mowed-em.*" Willie laughed hard, and the two men just shook their heads. "I made that one up, all by myself."

"I can believe it, Willie," Grandpa said. The

mail carrier waved and walked back to the street.

Willie laughed under his breath as he helped Grandpa install the modem. Computer jokes kept popping into his mind.

Willie's computer wasn't the biggest in the world, but he had lots of bytes of memory on his hard drive. He smiled when he remembered when the computer was new.

"A byte?" he had asked his dad. "What does a computer chew?"

"It's not like that," his dad answered. "Think about it like this: You measure how much you weigh in pounds. You measure how tall you are in inches. For a computer, the amount of information it can keep in its memory is measured in bytes."

Willie nodded. "I get it. Bytes, with a *y*."

Dad went on. "Your computer stores its bytes of memory on a hard drive. The hard drive records the information as a cassette tape records music."

Finally, Grandpa was ready. "This is where computer users call to talk to each other," Grandpa said as he showed Willie how to dial up the local computer bulletin board.

"Why don't they just use the phone like everyone else?"

"A bulletin board lets several of them talk to each other at the same time," explained Grandpa. "They can also leave each other messages and swap programs such as computer games."

"Games! I like computer games."

"Willie, you have to remember one important thing," Grandpa said. "Using a computer bulletin board is like going to town, and you need to be just as careful. You meet all kinds of people, some nice, some not so nice. If you see anything that you think might be bad, you tell me. OK?"

Willie nodded.

"When you call a computer bulletin board, the system operator keeps track of who you are and how often you call," explained Grandpa. "But you get to make up a name to use when you talk to other people on the network. That's the fun part!"

"Cool!" Willie typed in his real name and home phone number. Then the bulletin board asked for his "handle."

"That's the name you want others to call you," Grandpa said.

"What should I call myself?" Willie looked at the floor a minute, then said, "I know!" He typed out: *H-O-T W-H-E-E-L-S*.

"I couldn't have thought of a better handle myself," Grandpa said. "Why don't we see who's talking today?"

Willie clicked on the button called "Chat." The screen went blank for a second. Then lines of words appeared on the screen. A sentence or two would appear, separated from the other sentences by a colored bar. Willie decided that each section of words came from a different computer.

"The computers *are* talking to each other!" Willie said.

"Well, not really," Grandpa said. "There are people behind those messages."

Willie read:

gnat: hey, how about that game last night. the giants won again. :-)

bo: just wait. my team will get them next time.

tweedly: hey, do you guys always have to talk baseball? i mean, really, there's more to life than chasing some ball.

gnat: such as?

tweedly: such as *shopping.* :-)

bo: gag! :-(

---

gnat: double gag! :-(

"Why don't they use any capital letters?" Willie asked. "It seems like it would be easier to read if they did."

"On computer bulletin boards, using capital letters is like shouting. It's considered bad manners," Grandpa said. "If they want to emphasize something, they use those little starry things called asterisks. And they can add a sideways smiley [:-)] or frowning [:-( ] faces after their comments, as well."

Willie stared at the faces they had typed in sideways with their comments. "I see," he said. "So how do I talk to them?"

"Just type it there when you have something to say, then click the Send button," Grandpa said. He patted Willie on the shoulder, then went in the other room.

I've always got something to say, Willie thought. His heart pounded as he typed out a message and pressed the Send button:

hot wheels: why was the computer tired after going home?

Willie took a deep breath and waited to see if there would be any response. After a moment, he read:

tweedly: well, a newcomer. glad to have you, hot wheels. i give up, why was the computer tired after going home?

Willie grinned to himself as he typed in the answer:

Because it was a hard drive. :-)

Immediately, the others responded.

gnat: bad joke, but we're glad to have you here, hot wheels.

bo: aw, come on, gnat, it's miles better than your baseball jokes. :-) welcome, hot wheels.

tweedly: don't listen to these old goats, hot wheels. you have a real talent there.

The next afternoon, Chris and Maria Vargas stopped by. Willie told his computer jokes. Then he showed them the computer. "I know you can't stay long, but you've got to see this."

As they came in, Coco was standing on his hind legs, reaching for what looked like a ball of fuzz next to the computer. "Coco, leave that alone," Willie warned.

The fuzzy thing was attached to a wire leading to the computer. "What is it?" Maria asked.

"It's my computer mouse," Willie said, patting the fuzzy thing lying by the computer. "A mouse helps you choose things and move them around on a computer screen. Actually, the fuzzy part is just a cover, but Coco thinks it's a real mouse."

Willie switched the computer on. "First, you have to dial the bulletin-board number," he explained. "Then you look at the menu and choose which direction you go from there."

"Oh, it's a modem," Chris said.

The bulletin-board screen came on, but right away, Willie noticed that something was different. A message flashed at the bottom of the screen.

"Look, you've got a message in your mailbox!"

Willie clicked on the button that led them to Hot Wheels's mailbox. Instead of language he could understand, Willie found a series of numbers:

**8-15-23 4-15-5-19 1 3-15-13-16-21-20-5-18
5-1-20 1 16-9-26-26-1?**

"Look who it's signed by," Chris said.

At the bottom of the message were three letters:

g.o.d.

2

Who Is G.O.D.?

Chris and Maria looked at each other. Then they began to laugh. "Big joke, Willie," Chris said. "You set this up just for us, didn't you?"

Willie turned and looked at them. "Are you kidding? I have no idea what this code means or who G.O.D. is."

"Why, it's God, of course," Chris said.

"Yeah, right," Willie said. "God's going to leave a secret-code message for me on a computer."

"It could happen," Maria said.

"No, really," Chris said, "who has the initials G.O.D.?"

2—C.S.C. ·

"Nobody I know," Willie said. "But you know, if it's a handle, it could mean something else."

"Yeah, like **G**ood **O**ld **D**ude," Chris said.

"Or **G**ray **O**ld **D**onkey," Willie said. "So I guess it's probably an older person."

"Not necessarily," Maria said. "How about **G**et **O**ut **D**uck?"

"So I guess we can't know who it is just by these three initials," Willie said, almost to himself. "What else do we know?"

"Well, maybe we should figure out the code," Maria said. "There could be a clue hidden in it."

"It just looks like a bunch of numbers to me," Willie said.

"Well, the numbers have to stand for letters," Maria guessed. "Otherwise, we will never be able to understand the message."

"Yeah, but which letters are supposed to go with which numbers?" Chris asked.

Willie leaned back in his wheelchair. "Let's see, twenty-six letters in the alphabet . . . wait a minute. I've got an idea!" Willie reached on the shelf beside the computer and grabbed a pen and a piece of paper.

"We write out the alphabet from *A* to *Z*," he

explained as he scribbled. "Then we put numbers one through twenty-six above them like this:"

1 2 3 4 5 6 7 8 9 10 11 12 13 14 15 16 17 18 19
20 21 22 23 24 25 26
A B C D E F G H I J K L N M O P Q R S
T U V W X Y Z

Maria's eyes lighted up. "Yes, I get it," she said.

"I don't," Chris said. "What does it all mean?"

"Use your brain, brother," Maria teased. "One number for one letter?"

Chris stared at the paper blankly. Then his eyes widened. "Oh yeah! Let's write the message on the paper and see if your idea works."

They wrote out the numbered message Willie had received. Using the matching list of numbers and letters, they worked until they had a message they could understand.

"OK, here's the last word," Chris said. "Sixteen is the letter *P*, then 9 is *I*. Twenty-six is *Z*, then *Z* again, and the last letter is *A*."

"Pizza!" shouted Maria.

"Here's the message: 'How does a computer eat a pizza?' " Willie read.

Chris moaned. "It's a computer joke. Now I *know* you put the code on there."

Willie shrugged and threw his hands in the air. "I didn't. Really!"

"Well, who else likes computer jokes?" Maria asked.

Willie shrugged again. "You guys, Grandpa, and everyone on the computer bulletin board."

A car horn honked outside. "That's Mom," Chris said. "We have to go."

"And we still don't know who G.O.D. is," Maria said with a frown.

"If I come up with any ideas, I'll let you know," Chris said on his way out.

"In the meantime, maybe you can leave a message on the bulletin board for this G.O.D. person and get some more clues," Maria added.

"Right," Willie said. "I'll see you this week-end at the Shoebox."

Willie turned back to the computer screen. The secret code stared at him. "I don't know who you are, G.O.D., but I'm going to find out."

Willie thought for a long minute before he clicked on the button called "Mailbag." Then he typed out his message:

to: g.o.d.
from: hot wheels
2-25-20-5 2-25 2-25-20-5.
p.s. who are you, really?

Later that evening, the phone rang while Willie and Grandpa were doing the evening dishes. "I'll get it," Willie shouted. He pushed his wheelchair down the hall as fast as it would go.

"Hello, this is Willie Teller," he said to the phone, out of breath.

"Well, hello, Willie Teller. This is Gene Teller, your father. Remember me?"

"Dad!" Willie said. "Of course I remember you. You've only been gone three days."

"Well, that's good to know," Dad said.

"I've missed you," Willie said.

"Mom and I have missed you too. Just a few more days, and then we'll be headed home. What's going on around there?"

Willie told Dad about the modem and the computer bulletin board and especially about the coded message he had received.

"So you have no idea who this G.O.D. person is?" Dad asked.

Willie shook his head, then remembered they were talking on the phone. "Nope. I started making a list of people it could be, but some of the names seemed rather silly."

"Like whom?" Dad asked.

"Well, like Grandpa. He knows all about computers and was there when I was making the computer jokes, but it just doesn't seem like he would do this sort of thing."

"Well, don't strike anyone from your list until you're sure they couldn't have done it," Dad said. "What about your friends Maria and Chris? They have a computer."

"Yeah, but they didn't hear me tell the joke until after they were already over here. It has to be someone on the computer bulletin board."

"Well, I wish you luck," Dad said. "There's nothing like a good mystery to keep you busy thinking."

"Yeah, I just wish I could turn to the last page and find out who did it," Willie said. Dad laughed and passed the phone on to Mom. After a few more minutes, it was time to hang up. "OK, I love you. 'Bye-bye."

I'm glad Mom and Dad got to go on this trip, but I'll be even gladder when they get home, he thought.

"Willie, it's time for bed," Grandpa said later.

"Aw, Grandpa, can't I have just fifteen minutes more?" Willie was deep in a game of Thunder Toads on his computer and had almost made it to the fourth level.

"OK, fifteen minutes, then it's off to bed," Grandpa said.

Zaap! Willie's Thunder Toad disappeared, and the words *Game Over* appeared. He reached for the switch, then decided to check the bulletin board one more time.

He dialed in and pulled up the bulletin board. There was another message for him.

He grinned and clicked on the Mailbag button.

23-12-3-13   20   20-8   2-12-12-20-14   1-18-4.
i   2-14   23-20-3-8-14-7   u   12-14-7   20-13   14-
4   13   7-12-4   u   8-22   10-14-4   19   8-18.   i
8-16   20   8-18   6-18-13   u   7-14   19-14.
g.o.d.

All right, he thought, *this will be easy. Wait a minute, it's not the same code as before!* He gritted his teeth. *Well, if G.O.D. wants to make it tough, I can take it.*

3

At the Shoebox

Willie was always glad to go to church. Every week, he and his friends met in the Shoebox. Their class had more fun than anyone else's. Mrs. Shue made sure of that.

That's one reason why Willie was smiling when Grandpa pulled Willie's wheelchair from the trunk of the car. He jumped in and led the way across the church parking lot.

"See you later, Grandpa." Willie steered his wheelchair down the hall at high speed. Even before he got there, he could hear singing. Willie joined in while he was still in the hallway.

Willie knew that his voice wasn't that great, but he made up for it by singing as loud as he could. "I've got peace like a river, I've got peace like a river, I've got peace like a river in my sooool." It wasn't until he wheeled through the door that he realized the others had stopped singing.

"Ulp!" Willie said, suddenly embarrassed. Sitting in the second row, Maria and DeeDee started to giggle. Chris, sitting in his usual spot by the aisle in the back row, grinned and gave Willie a thumbs-up sign.

"Welcome, Willie!" Mrs. Shue acted as if nothing was wrong. "You're sure in a good mood this morning!"

"Yes, Mrs. Shue!" Willie grinned back at her.

"Then let's get started." Mrs. Shue looked around at the kids in the Shoebox. "Who has had something special happen to them this week?" Willie looked down, but Chris nudged him. "Tell her," he said to Willie.

"No. You tell her."

"Tell me what, Willie?" Mrs. Shue looked back at them.

"Willie's been getting secret messages," Maria said.

"Oh, really," Mrs. Shue said. "What kind of messages?"

Maria told the group about Willie's modem and the secret message they had read on the computer screen. "The message came from G.O.D."

"You mean the one up in heaven?" Sammy asked, sitting on the other side of Chris.

"Of course not," DeeDee said, sitting with Maria. "God doesn't use computers."

"Why not?" Chris asked. "He invented them too."

"He did not," Jenny said. "A man did—a scientist."

"So who gave him the idea? God can do anything He wants to do—even send us messages on computers." Chris folded his hands over his chest and stuck his chin out at Jenny and DeeDee.

"He can *not*," Jenny said.

"Can *so*," Chris shot back.

"Children, arguing will get us nowhere," Mrs. Shue said. "But it is a good reason to discuss our lesson today. Sammy, what are we studying?"

"We're studying Luke 11—the part about prayer."

"Jesus was teaching His disciples to pray. DeeDee, why do you think Jesus did that?

Why was it important for the disciples to learn how to pray?"

"Because they needed to know how to ask God for all the good stuff they needed, or they wouldn't get it," DeeDee said.

"That's silly," Chris said. "God knows what we're thinking before we say anything. Why does He need us to say anything? Why doesn't He just answer our prayer before we ask?"

"Who can answer that?" Mrs. Shue said. Maria raised her hand.

"Sometimes I know you want the mashed potatoes when we're sitting at the dinner table, Chris," Maria said. "But I wait to hear you ask for them before I pass them. That's the polite thing to do."

Jenny raised her hand. "And God wants to hear more than what we want. My mom said He's just like a parent. He doesn't want us to act like He's some sort of gift machine; He wants to hear that we love Him."

"But remember that God does want to give you good things, just like your parents do," Mrs. Shue added. "Sometimes they don't give you what you ask. Sometimes they have something else planned for you. But listen to this: 'Ask and it will be given to you; seek and you will find; knock and the door will be opened to you' (Luke 11, verse 9)."

DeeDee raised her hand again. "But that still doesn't mean that God can talk to you over your computer."

Mrs. Shue shrugged and held up her hands. "What do you think, class? Can you think of any unusual ways God talked to people in the Bible?"

Sammy raised his hand. "He talked to Moses through a burning bush."

"And He used a small voice to talk to Elijah," Maria said.

"He wrote on the wall at that feast in Babylon," Chris added.

DeeDee stood up. "But that doesn't mean He's talking to Willie on his computer."

Mrs. Shue looked at Willie. "What do you think, Willie?"

Willie was silent for a long while. Then he said, "I got another message."

Everyone listened.

"I got a longer message after Chris and Maria left Thursday night," Willie said. "At first, I thought it would be just like the other one. I thought I could just switch the numbers to letters and get the message. But this one was different.

"This code had letters in it too. After I trans-
lated the numbers to letters, I put the old letters
and the new letters all together. I'll show you."

Willie rolled his wheelchair to the front and
began writing on the blackboard:

WLCM T TH BLLTN BRD. iV BN
WTCHNG u LNG TM ND M GLD u HV
JND S HR. i HP T HR FRM u GN SN.
g.o.d.

"Weird," Sammy said under his breath.

"That doesn't look like anything God would
say," DeeDee said.

"How do you know?" Chris snapped back.

"Chris, DeeDee, settle down!" Mrs. Shue
said. "Actually, that's one of the reasons Jesus
taught people through parables. He said things
that many people didn't understand the first
time. But if they were really looking for answers, they could figure it out."

"But this doesn't make any sense!" DeeDee said.

"I haven't figured it out yet," Willie said, "but
I think there is a pattern."

"I see it," Maria said. "The letters that G.O.D. left in the code are vowels, and the numbers that change to letters are all consonants."

"The message is there, just like Mrs. Shue said," Willie said. "We just have to really want to figure it out."

"But I do want to!" Chris said. "I just can't—wait a minute! I see it! The first word is *'Welcome!'* See?"

"Right!" Willie said. "Only the vowels are missing. Only words made up of vowels have them."

The Shoebox Kids worked on the code until they had the entire message:

Welcome to the bulletin board. I've been watching you a long time and am glad you have joined us here. I hope to hear from you again soon.
G.O.D.

"Well, Willie, it looks like your computer pen pal is inviting you to send him another message," said Mrs. Shue. "I hope you don't let him or her down."

"But that doesn't prove that G.O.D. is—" DeeDee said.

Chris rolled his eyes.

That evening, Willie sat in front of his computer console, staring at the empty screen. For a long time, he didn't know what he should write, though it seemed important that he say *something*. Finally, he wrote:

---

to: g.o.d.
from: hot wheels
today at church we talked about prayer. though i'm pretty sure you're not the god that we pray to, i thought you might have an opinion about it. after all, there's not much difference between what we're doing right now and when i pray to god before i go to sleep at night. maybe the only difference is that i can see god working in my life, while you're just a pen pal. anyway, i just want you to know that i'm glad you're my friend and that you take the time to send messages to me like this. thanks.
p.s. what flavor of ice cream do you like? or does g.o.d. like ice cream?

Willie looked at the message for a long moment, pressed the Send button on his computer, switched it off, and headed for bed.

4

The Vanishing Library Book

"Hello, this is Willie Teller," Willie said as he answered the telephone Monday morning.

"Willie, this is Mrs. Hutchinson at the Mill Valley Public Library. You have an overdue book—*Dog Heroes of World War Two*. It was due two weeks ago."

"I—I don't think I have that book anymore," Willie said. But he didn't remember returning it, either.

"Well, Willie, I hope you understand that if you lose a book, you are responsible for paying for it. In this case, we are talking about ten dollars, plus a five-dollar fine."

"Fifteen dollars!" Willie knew he didn't have that kind of money.

"I'm sorry, but in two days you must either return the book or pay the money," Mrs. Hutchinson said.

Willie hung up the receiver and stared at the wall. Where could the book be? Where could he get the money to replace it? He wheeled back down to his room and decided that he would search the room, even though in his heart he knew it wasn't there.

Fifteen dollars! The more Willie thought about it, the more miserable he became. Hot tears began to fall as he struggled through the last shelf of his bookcase.

"Willie, what's wrong?" Grandpa stood in the doorway with a concerned look on his face.

"I've lost a library book, and now they say I owe them fifteen dollars," Willie sobbed.

"I could give you the money," Grandpa said.

"Well . . . that wouldn't really be fair," Willie said. "You didn't lose the book."

"Did you pray about it?" Grandpa asked.

Immediately, Willie thought of Mrs. Shue

and her talk about prayer. "Ask and it shall be given unto you," Mrs. Shue had read. "Seek and you shall find."

Is God really concerned about my missing library book? Even if it's my fault? Willie wondered. He looked up at Grandpa. "Thanks, Grandpa."

When Grandpa left his room, Willie bowed his head and folded his hands. "God, a lot of things have been happening in the last few days to make me wonder about You. It's my fault I lost that library book. But would You help me find it anyway? I don't like to ask for help, even from Grandpa. But Mrs. Shue says I can ask You for help anytime, so I am. Thanks for being my friend. In Jesus' name, amen."

Willie wondered why he'd made that last statement—*Thanks for being my friend*—and wondered if it had anything to do with his messages on the computer.

The only difference is that I see God working in my life, and you're just a pen pal, he had written in the message to G.O.D. the night before. Did God work in his life? Could he see that?

Through the window, he saw the mail carrier walk along the sidewalk and come toward their house. Mr. Davis carried a brown package, a lot like the one the modem had come in. A strange chill went down Willie's spine. He raced in his wheelchair to pull the door open.

"Got a package for you, Willie," the mail carrier said. "Is it another modem? Or maybe a computer game?"

"I don't know," Willie said. He reached out eagerly for the package. On the front, it was clearly addressed to Willie Teller and had the right address. In the upper left corner, where the return address should have been, it simply said "G.O.D."

"God sent me my book back," Willie whispered. He tore the package open. Inside was the missing library book.

"What?" The mail carrier cupped his hand by his ear. "I didn't quite catch that."

"I said, God sent me my library book back," Willie said, grinning ear to ear. "G.O.D. is really God." He showed the mail carrier the return address on the package.

The mail carrier looked surprised. "Now, Willie, I wouldn't go jumping to any conclusions there. I mean, just because the initials *G.O.D.* are on the package—"

"But, Mr. Davis, you don't understand. Only my grandfather, Mrs. Hutchinson at the library, and God knew that I had lost this book. Who else could it be?"

"Well, Willie, over the years, I've seen God work in the lives of many people. And most times, God answers prayer by using those of us who claim to be Christians. After all, that's what we're here for, isn't it?"

I still think it was a miracle, Willie said to himself. The way he explained it to Mrs. Hutchinson, she almost believed that angels had placed the book directly in Willie's hands.

As he wheeled toward the library exit, he saw DeeDee coming in.

"DeeDee, I saw a miracle!" Willie said.

"Oh yeah?" DeeDee raised one eyebrow. "What did you see? Did Coco turn into a Shetland pony?"

"No, a *real* miracle," Willie said without hesitating. "I lost a library book and asked God to help me find it, and He did."

"Now which God is this? Is that G.O.D.—or the real One in heaven?"

"I think they may be the same one," Willie said quietly.

DeeDee shook her head. "No way."

Willie told her about the package with the G.O.D. initials on it.

"Didn't anyone ever tell you that God can use people to answer your prayers as well?" DeeDee pushed her face close to Willie's.

"Well . . ."

"And here's something else to think about," DeeDee said. "Chris and Maria's computer has a modem too."

Willie frowned at DeeDee skeptically. "How do you know?"

DeeDee smiled as if she had just won a race. "Their mom and my mom were talking. Mrs. Vargas told her about the messages you've been getting. She said that in the two years since they got their modem, they have never gotten messages like that."

Willie looked at her silently, deep in thought. "You're sure about this?"

"Sure I'm sure," DeeDee said. "But don't take my word for it. Why don't you check it out yourself?"

Willie didn't answer. *All right, I will,* he said silently.

"Well, how goes the mystery?" Dad asked

that evening on the phone.

"Not too good," Willie said. "Every time I think I have it figured out, another clue makes me change my mind."

"Well, sometimes it helps to just lay all the facts out," Dad said. "Tell me about it."

"OK, first let me describe the mystery person," Willie said. "The mystery person is a he or she who goes by the 'handle' of G.O.D., whatever that means. They have sent me two different number codes. The first was a computer riddle, something that only Grandpa, Chris and Maria, and the people on the bulletin board know that I was doing.

"The second code was a personal message that welcomed me to the bulletin board and said they hoped to hear from me again. They also said that they had been 'watching me a long time.'"

"So it's someone who knows you, even if you don't really know them," Dad said.

"And they knew enough about me to return my library book," Willie added.

"OK, who do you think it might be?" Dad said.

"First." Willie hesitated for an embarrassed few seconds. "There's you and Mom."

Dad chuckled in response. "OK," he said.

"After all, I could have left the library book in your van, and you could have mailed it back from where you are."

"Well, maybe. Look at the postmark on the package."

"OK." Willie lifted the brown paper and looked at the postal mark in the corner. "It says it was mailed from here in town, but you could have mailed it before you left."

"Look at the date. We left on the fifteenth."

Willie looked at it. "OK, you're clean. It was mailed on the seventeenth."

"Thanks, detective." Dad chuckled again. "At least you're finding out who couldn't have done it."

"And then there's Grandpa and Maria and Chris and all the people on the computer bulletin board."

"Well, here's something that might help. Take a look at the handwriting on the package."

Willie looked at the package again. "Yeah, it's got handwriting on it."

"All you have to do is—"

"Match the handwriting, and I have the mystery person!" Willie finished the thought. "Thanks, Dad. I love you."

"I love you too, Willie. Happy hunting."

Willie hung up the phone and smiled to himself. The answer was so simple. All he had to do was get samples of the suspects' handwriting and compare. And he knew just where to start.

5

Writing on the ... Wall?

The mystery is almost solved, Willie thought to himself. He rolled into his bedroom and went straight to his closet. Under his clothes, in the far corner of his closet, he kept a shoebox. In that box, he stored the neat special things his mother was always wanting to throw away. He lifted the lid and looked inside.

First, he saw the glittery rock he had found with his dad in Mount Pleasant Park last summer. He lifted a plastic bag and held it up to the light. Inside was the dried tarantula he had found on their trip to Arizona.

He dug past a broken marble and three plastic spacemen. Finally, he found what he was looking for.

Willie pulled a postcard from the bottom of the box. The picture showed a kid skiing on Lake Joyful. He turned it over and looked at the message: "Hi, Willie, I'm having a great time. I got sunburned yesterday. Tell the other Shoebox kids Hi for me. See you soon. Chris."

It was addressed to: "Willie Teller, 6322 Tradewinds Lane, Mill Valley."

Willie stared at the address. He looked at the brown package wrapping in his lap. Then he looked at the address again.

They're not even close, Willie thought. *The handwriting is someone else's.*

"Well, Chris," Willie said. "You'll be pleased to know that you're not a suspect anymore."

"What's that?"

Willie jumped, but it was only Grandpa. "Who are you talking to, Willie?"

"I'm just trying to solve a mystery, Grandpa." Willie smiled up at him and quickly put the postcard back in the shoebox. *You're next*, he thought.

"Grandpa, did you ever write Mom and Dad any

letters?" Willie put the shoebox back in his closet.

"Letters? I don't think so. I've never been much of a writer. Why?"

Willie frowned and looked at the floor. "How about Christmas cards?"

"Oh, sure," he said cheerily. "We send you and your mom and dad a Christmas card every year."

"You do?" Willie's hopes brightened. "Maybe Mom has kept one around here."

Willie wheeled down the hall toward the garage door, and Grandpa trailed behind.

"Yeah, your grandmother always signs our names and gets them out the day after Thanksgiving," said Grandpa. "But knowing your mother, I doubt if she's kept last year's Christmas cards until now. It's June, boy."

Willie opened the garage door and looked inside. He realized that Grandpa was right. Mom would have thrown them away months ago. Besides, what use were they if Grandma was the one who signed their names?

Willie felt Grandpa grab the wheelchair and spin it around so that Willie faced him.

"Now, you young pup, are you going to tell me what this is about, or am I going to have to tickle it out of you?" He poked at Willie's ribs and tickled him until Willie escaped.

"It's nothing, Grandpa," Willie said, wheeling away, back to the living room. "Like I said, I'm trying to solve a mystery."

"It's that secret-code business, isn't it?" Grandpa raised one eyebrow. "Well, what can I do to help?"

Willie looked at Grandpa silently. *Is it smart to let a suspect help you on your case?* he asked himself. *One thing he could do wouldn't hurt.*

"I—I think I can handle it myself," Willie said. He saw Grandpa's shoulders slump in disappointment. "That is, Grandpa, if you would do one thing for me."

"What's that?"

Willie rolled over to the cabinet in the corner and opened a drawer. "Take this pen and paper, and write my name and address on it."

"That's it?" Grandpa looked surprised. He shrugged and leaned on the table as he wrote out Willie's name and address. "Here you go." He turned and gave the paper to Willie.

Willie held up the paper and the brown wrapper. He looked at one, and then the other, for a long while, then dropped both arms to his lap.

"You're OK," he said, taking a deep breath.

"I'm OK. Does that mean I'm not a suspect anymore?" Grandpa asked.

Willie nodded. "I've got one more person to check, though. May I invite Chris and Maria over again?"

Grandpa chuckled. "Only if it helps you solve this case."

"Do you have any more computer jokes for us?" Chris asked as they entered the front door.

"I'm not in a joking mood," Willie said. "This mystery is getting nowhere." He told them about getting the library book in the package.

"So G.O.D. knew about your library book," said Maria. "Great. Now, all you have to do is find out whose handwriting is on the package."

"That's what I've been trying to do," Wille said quietly. He turned to Chris. "By the way, your handwriting didn't match. You are no longer a suspect."

"What about my handwriting?" Maria asked. "Am I still a suspect?"

"I got a sample of Chris's handwriting from that postcard he sent me when you guys were on vacation. I didn't have a sample of yours."

"So my sister could still be the mystery

person," Chris said. "How scary." Maria stuck her tongue out.

"I'll take you off my suspect list if you can pass two tests, Maria," Willie said, pulling out a sheet of paper and a pen.

"You want me to write your name and address," she said matter-of-factly. She leaned over the table and scribbled for a long moment. "There. Satisfied?" She handed the paper back to Willie.

In response, Willie took the brown package and held it up next to the paper, just as he had done with Grandpa's handwriting. He was silent for a long moment. Chris and Maria watched him until they couldn't stand it any longer.

"Well?" Maria finally said.

"Mmm . . . close but . . . no." Willie looked over at Maria. "You make funny *R*s."

Chris laughed. "That's not the only thing funny about her."

"One more question for the two of you," Willie said, serious again. "DeeDee saw me at the library and said that you guys have a modem on your computer."

Chris and Maria looked at each other. "Yeah, so?"

"Why didn't you tell me about it before this?"

"You didn't ask," Chris said.

"What do you mean?" Willie said.

"It doesn't work, Willie. My dad disconnected it about six months ago," Maria said. "He was afraid of getting computer viruses."

"Computer *what*?" Willie asked.

"You know, like diseases?" Chris said.

"Computers don't get diseases. Even I know that, Chris," Willie said.

"Well, they're not really diseases," explained Maria. "They're just computer programs weird people write that mess up your computer. You can pick them up from other computers."

"Like a cold," Chris added.

"Since our modem didn't work, we didn't want to spoil your fun with your modem. So we didn't say anything."

"So are we both suspects—or what?" Chris asked.

"As far as I can tell at this point, you're not," Willie said. "What do we do now?"

"We could go over to the post office. We could check out everyone's handwriting as they send out their mail," Maria suggested.

"I don't think the post office would let us hang around there," Willie said.

"Well, how about the grocery store? We could look over people's shoulders as they write their checks," Chris offered. "Besides, I'm hungry."

"I don't think anyone will be writing checks with my name on them," Willie said. "Why don't I make us some peanut-butter-and-jelly sandwiches? We can think while we take a break."

Willie rolled into the kitchen while Maria and Chris waited in the living room. Maria spotted the computer and switched it on.

"When was the last time you checked for messages?" she asked Willie, in the other room.

"Last night. Nothing."

Maria walked into the kitchen. "Well, you should have checked today. There's one there now, and it's a whopper."

CHAPTER

6

Another Clue

"What did you say?" Willie asked suddenly from the kitchen.

"I said you've got another message," Maria responded. "It's long, and it's big, and I don't read other people's mail. So come in here and read it before I explode."

Willie wiped the peanut butter from his hands onto his pants and wheeled into the computer room. Maria and Chris stood behind him as he read the message:

dear hot wheels:

you're right, i'm not who you think i am, although i talk to him regularly. prayer makes a big difference. god is more than someone to turn to when you have a problem or are in trouble. he's the very best friend you could ever have. i know that you don't like to ask for help, but everyone needs help sometime, even g.o.d. i believe that you will figure out this mystery. you're really too smart for me. so to keep it interesting, here's another clue:

Nt d'cieurw uxw xew'n ua eixjt ei's.

"What is *that*?" Maria asked and pointed at the new code.

"What happened to the numbers?" Chris asked.

"G.O.D. knew that we had figured out the other codes," Willie said. "So we get a new one."

"I *liked* the numbers," Chris said, staring at the screen. "I could figure them out. I don't think I can figure this one out."

"Oh, come on, Chris," Maria said. "We haven't even tried yet. We can do it."

Willie went back to the kitchen and finished making the sandwiches. Chris and Maria stared at the computer screen. When he returned to the room, Chris and Maria just shook their heads.

"The other codes made some sense," Maria

said. "This one doesn't seem to have a pattern."

"It's got a pattern," Willie said. "It's just different from the ones we've already done." Coco came in and stood on his back legs, reaching up toward Willie's sandwich. "Here, boy," Willie threw a piece high in the air. Coco took a couple of steps backward and caught the sandwich piece in midair.

"Good boy," Willie said.

"Hey, what happened to your fancy mouse cover?" Chris lifted the plastic computer mouse off its pad.

"Hey, where is it?" Willie asked. He turned to Coco, who sat wagging his tail and facing them. "Coco, what did you do with it?" Coco whimpered and lay down on the ground.

"I know where he hides things." Willie headed across the living room to the coat closet. The door stood partially open. "Coco, come here." Coco stood and whined. Willie opened the closet door.

"My mouse cover," he wailed. Coco watched as Willie lifted the shredded mouse cover up where the others could see it. Now it looked more like a dead mouse.

"Bad dog!" Willie reached out and swatted Coco. Coco yelped and lay on the floor. "Come on. You're going outside." Willie rolled to the back door and opened it. Coco rushed out.

"Willie, don't you think you were a little hard on Coco?" Maria asked when he came back.

"Yeah, it's just a mouse cover,"Chris said.

"Coco chews up everything," Willie said under his breath. "He should know better." Willie tried to change the subject. "What do you want to do now?"

"Well, Chris and I have to go home pretty soon," Maria said. "Why don't we get a copy of this code, and we can take it home and work on it."

Willie shrugged. "I can't think of a better idea. Maybe one of us will run into G.O.D.'s handwriting somewhere."

Chris spoke up. "I'll talk to Dad and see if he knows who runs the computer bulletin board. Maybe they can give us some information about G.O.D."

Maria copied down the code, folded it neatly, and stuffed it into her pocket. Just then, a car horn sounded out front. "That's Mom," Maria announced.

"Call me tonight if you think of anything," Willie called after them.

Willie turned back to the computer and the mysterious new code:

Nt d'cieurw uxw xew'n ua eixjt ei's.

There has to be some sort of pattern, he thought. *But what is it?* Willie wrote out the alphabet like they had done the first time to see if it helped. It didn't.

This one has vowels and consonants both, so that's no help, he thought. *But I do know that all words include at least one vowel. That's a start.*

Willie wrote out the two two-letter words: *Nt* and *ua. What two-letter words do I know?* He wrote out *is, of, to, he, my, an, as.* But it didn't help. *What about the words with the punctuation mark in them? The marks must be part of the code.*

What would happen if. . . Willie looked at the computer keyboard, then back at the code. Slowly, he pushed the keys that were *just to the right* of those letters on the keyboard. Like magic, words began to form before his eyes.

My favorite ice cream is rocky road.

Willie's mouth dropped open. "I'm a *genius*! Coco, I did it!" When Coco didn't answer, Willie looked around, then remembered he had put

Coco outside. Thinking about the scolding he had given Coco, he started feeling bad.

Willy wheeled to the back door and called, "Coco!" He waited a long moment, but there was no answer.

He saw Grandpa pulling weeds in the garden. "Grandpa, have you seen Coco?"

"What do you mean?" Grandpa stood and wiped the sweat from his face. "Isn't Coco inside with you?"

"No, he was bad, so I put him in the backyard."

Grandpa walked up to the back door. "I wish you would have told me," Grandpa said. "I've been moving a lot of things through the backyard. The gate's open."

"Coco," they both called. "Coco, come here." They waited a long time, but there was no answer.

"Oh no, he ran away," Willie said. *And it's all my fault*, he thought.

Just then, they heard a car's tires screech on the street in front of their house.

CHAPTER 7

Where's Coco?

Willie's heart leapt to his throat as he heard the tires squeal. Grandpa raced around the corner of the house, and Willie turned and went back through the house.

Willie plastered his face to the front window and breathed a sigh of relief. Some kids were playing baseball in the street. A car zoomed past them. "Stay out of the street," the driver yelled at one boy.

He watched as Grandpa asked the kids if they had seen Coco. Two of them shook their heads. The boy who had been yelled at said something that Willie couldn't hear clearly and pointed down the street. Grandpa nodded, waved a thanks, and turned back to the house.

"One of them saw Coco about a half-hour ago," Grandpa said as he came in the front door. "He probably hasn't gone very far."

Willie looked up with tears in his eyes. "It's my fault, Grandpa."

Grandpa cradled Willie's head against his chest. "There, there, now. It's just as much my fault as it is yours. I left the gate open."

"But I yelled at him," Willie said. "I hit him."

"Well, you said he did something bad. I know that doesn't excuse you for hitting him, but I'm sure Coco isn't mad at you. He loves you, and he knows that this is his home. I doubt if he's gone very far." Grandpa tilted Willie's face toward his. "Has Coco ever run away before?"

"Never," Willie sniffed.

"I'll tell you what. I'll drive around the neighborhood and look. Maybe I'll see him, and he'll hop right in the car."

"What about me?" Willie asked.

"One of us has to be here in case he decides to come back," Grandpa explained.

Willie nodded, although he would rather be

out looking for Coco.

Losing Coco made Willie forget how happy he was to break the latest code from G.O.D. He tried playing with his computer, but he couldn't concentrate. Every five minutes, he would wheel to the back door and call for Coco, then go to the front porch and look down the street.

An hour went by. Finally, Willie heard Grandpa's car drive in the garage. *Please, God,* he prayed, *please let Coco be with Grandpa.* The door opened, however, and Grandpa entered. Without Coco.

"I—I don't understand," Willie said.

"I'm sorry, Willie. I didn't see him. I covered the whole neighborhood."

"But I don't understand," Willie repeated.

Grandpa bent down in front of Willie. "What don't you understand?"

"I prayed and asked God to let you find Coco," Willie said, almost in tears. "He answered my prayer about the library book. Why didn't He answer this prayer?"

Grandpa let out his breath and looked at the floor for a minute before replying. "Willie, you have to understand that God is God. He has His own reasons for the things He does. Sometimes,

He lets things happen that we understand much later. Sometimes, things happens that we won't understand until we get to heaven."

Grandpa stood up. "And sometimes, we make mistakes, and He allows us to live with the results of those mistakes. That's how we learn, as painful as it may be."

Willie's stomach did flip-flops from everything that had happened. He felt angry, sad, and worried about Coco. Even though he knew better, he felt angry at God, too, for not bringing Coco back. Most of all, he felt angry at himself.

"What—what do we do now, Grandpa?" he said finally.

"Well, I think we should just wait and see if Coco comes home. It'll be dark in about two hours. Let's see if Coco gets homesick about then."

Two hours came and went, and Coco didn't return. As it got darker and darker outside, Willie grew more and more worried. He jumped when the phone rang.

"Hello, this is Willie Teller," he answered.

"Willie, this is Chris," he heard the voice on the phone say. "Did you have any more luck with the code?"

"Yeah, I solved it," Willie said without enthusiasm.

"You solved it! That's great!" Chris said. "But you don't sound too happy."

"I'm not. Coco's run away," Willie said.

"Oh no!" Chris said. Willie heard his voice muffle as he told someone else about Coco. Then Maria came on the line.

"Willie, we'll call the other Shoebox Kids. If Coco's not back by morning, we'll all be there. We'll search until we find Coco!"

The first thing Willie did the next morning was to stick his head out the back door. "Coco, here, Coco." But there was no answer. When he didn't see anything up or down the street out front, Willie called Chris and Maria.

Before long, Mrs. Shue's car pulled up out front. All the Shoebox Kids were ready to search.

"Let's start with a plan," Mrs. Shue said. She laid out a map of the town. "Mill Valley isn't very big, so if we work in pairs, we can cover everything on this side of the river this morning. "

"A dog that small is not likely to go farther than that," Grandpa said as he handed out sack lunches to everyone.

"Willie and I will look downtown," Chris said, nodding to Willie. "That will make it easier for Willie and me to get around." Willie self-consciously played with the rails on his wheelchair.

"Well, if that's everything—" Mrs. Shue said.

"Wait!" Willie held up his hand. "I almost forgot." He wheeled back to the computer room and pulled out a large slip of paper.

"I made this last night on my computer," Willie said, unfolding it. The group read the poster Willie had created: "Dog Lost." In the middle of the poster was a drawing that looked a lot like Coco.

"I thought this might help," Willie said.

"It will," Mrs. Shue said, giving him a hug. "We'll find Coco. Let's stop by the church and make copies of the poster. Then we can put them up all over town."

Willie and Chris rode with Grandpa, while Mrs. Shue took the others. "I'll be back to check on you," Grandpa called after they were unloaded downtown.

"Don't worry about us, Grandpa," Willie said. "We'll be fine."

Willie was right. Mill Valley was small enough that many people knew each other, and almost everyone knew Willie.

"Willie, do you realize how many people around here could be G.O.D.?" Chris said as they entered a grocery store. "It seems like everyone knows you."

"Did your dad know anything about the computer bulletin board?" Willie asked.

"Only that they don't give out any information about people who use the bulletin board. It's against the law," Chris said.

"Well, there's another dead end," Willie said. After asking permission to put their poster on the store's yellow bulletin board, Chris began tacking it into place.

"Boy, there are sure a lot of cool things for sale up here," he said. "Look, here's an ad for a sailboat."

"Where?" Willie looked to where Chris pointed. Willie read: "Windjammer sailboat, used very little, $1,000. Call 555-1123. Mill Valley."

"Oh, well. We don't have that much money," Chris said as he pushed the last thumbtack into the corner of the poster. "Let's go."

"Wait." Willie held up his hand and looked at the ad. "Can you get that card down?"

"I don't think we're supposed to do that," Chris said.

"I just want to look at it," Willie said.

Chris shrugged and untacked the card with the sailboat ad. He gave the card to Willie. Willie looked at the ad for a long time, then pulled the wrinkled brown package wrapper from the backpack on his chair.

He held the card next to the package. Chris held his breath. "It's a match," Willie said finally. "This ad is from G.O.D."

8

Closer and Closer

"Are you sure?" Chris asked. He pressed closer and looked at the package and then at the card.

"Sure," Willie said. "Look at the word *Wind-jammer* here on the card. Now look at the word *Tradewinds* on the package. *Wind* is the same."

"I guess so," Chris said, not too sure.

"Now look at the town—*Mill Valley*."

Chris studied them. "Now, that looks the same." He looked up at Willie. "What next?"

Willie took a pen and wrote the phone number on the package from the ad. "Let's call this and see who answers."

Willie and Chris put the ad back on the bulletin board and found a pay phone outside the store. The phone was too high for Willie to reach it, so Chris called.

"No answer," he reported. "Let's try again later."

They wandered the main portion of downtown all morning but found no sign of Coco. Willie asked people he met if they had seen the little dog. He even showed them the poster. But no one could help.

After lunch with Grandpa, Willie and Chris decided to put their last two posters up in the library and post office.

Mrs. Hutchinson was at the front desk when Willie and Chris came in the front door. Willie felt a little nervous, but he rolled up to her and smiled. "Can we put up a poster about my lost dog?"

"You mean that cute little dog that always follows you around is gone? Why, of course."

Maybe Mrs. Hutchinson isn't such a mean person after all, Willie thought as he pushed in the tacks. *To keep the library going, I guess she has to make people return their books or pay for them.*

The post office was easier. While Chris put the poster up, Willie looked past the desk toward the back of the building.

"What are you looking for?" the man in front asked.

"Just wanted to see if Mr. Davis, my mail carrier, is here," Willie said.

"George is on his rounds. He'll be in soon," the man said.

"I just heard on the news that there's a bad summer storm coming in," Grandpa said when they got back in the car. "I'm going to take you boys home. Then I need to help Mrs. Shue round up the rest of the kids."

"But what about Coco?" Willie asked.

"Coco will just have to take care of himself for a little while longer," Grandpa said.

"Maybe Coco is already home," Chris said hopefully.

Coco wasn't there. "Want to try that phone number again?" Chris asked. Willie lifted the phone and dialed the number from the ad. He listened while the phone rang once, then clicked. Suddenly, he heard a high-pitched squeal.

Willie held the phone away from his ear. "What's *that*?" he said.

Chris leaned forward and listened. "It's the sound a modem makes!" He grabbed the phone and hung up.

"What are you doing?" Willie asked. Chris rushed to the computer and turned it on.

"It's a modem, get it? Someone—G.O.D., if you are right—is using their modem to get into the bulletin board."

Willie's eyes widened. "So they're on the bulletin board right now!"

"Want to talk screen to screen with the mystery person?"Chris asked.

As the bulletin board came on, Willie saw that he had no messages. He clicked the Chat button and began to read:

gnat: we just can't afford it.

bo: yeah, but the state inspectors aren't going to let us open the new stadium without wheelchair ramps!

gnat: i realize that there are laws, but there are always ways to get around those kinds of things. i mean, we're just a little town . . .

Willie and Chris watched for a few minutes, without seeing any mention of G.O.D. Just when Willie was about to switch off the computer, he saw something.

g.o.d.: gnat, when are you going to start thinking about someone other than yourself? think of all the good things you have going for you.

gnat: yeah, i guess so.

Willie didn't hesitate. He typed in his response and pressed Enter.

hot wheels: i have something to complain about.

A comment came in at once.

gnat: well, it's the newcomer. ok, what's your problem?

Willie typed back:

hot wheels: three things, really. i want to know how someone like me can get to see baseball games without wheelchair ramps.

gnat: what are you talking about?

g.o.d.: the kid's a wheelchair jockey.

bo: well, ok, what's second on your list?

hot wheels: what is this bulletin board good for except for wasting time? i mean, can a kid use it to help find his lost dog?

g.o.d.: you lost your dog?

hot wheels: the posters are all over town.

bo: yeah, i think i remember seeing one today. real sorry, kid.

g.o.d.: well, i think letting us know is a good start. what's number three?

hot wheels: number three is, who are you guys, really? how does one get to talk to g.o.d. face to face?

Willie's face felt hot as he waited for a response. Finally, it came:

gnat: ho, ho, ho. that's a good one. :-)

bo: tough luck, kid.

g.o.d.: the whole reason behind the bulletin board is so people can speak their minds without having to let people know who they are.

---

hot wheels: that's not fair.

---

g.o.d.: that's fair, and it's life. the best you can hope for is another message in your mailbox or maybe to bump into someone at the ice-cream store. don't think we don't care, but we take our privacy seriously.

Willie pushed himself away from his computer in disgust.

"Well, at least they were nice for the first two questions," Chris offered. "Maybe you should check and see if there are any other messages."

"There weren't any when we dialed in," Willie said.

"Well, it won't hurt to check again, will it?"

Willie shrugged, still angry. His anger disappeared suddenly when he saw the message that awaited him in his mailbox:

6]9]7] 2]8]9'9' 3'8]6]3' 3/9]3/9] 8]6/ 5]6'3]
9]9'3' 5'1'4'1'5'3] 3'9]2]6/ 5]6'3] 2'5]4]3]3]5].

9

Into the Storm

Chris whistled his surprise. "That's some code. Where does he come up with all of this?"

Willie was silent for a minute. "It looks hard, but I have an idea." He looked down at his keyboard. "I never told you how I solved the last code, did I?"

Before Chris could answer, Willie heard a knock and someone shout from the front room.

"Hey, anybody home?" It was Maria.

"Go away," Chris yelled.

"Come on in, Maria," Willie said. "Is everyone else back too?"

"No, just me. DeeDee's mom picked her up,

and I told Mom to meet us over here." She looked at the boys, then at the computer. "What's going on?"

"I was just about to explain how I figured out the last code," Willie said. "It was totally different from the number codes from before. So I just looked at the letters and other marks on the computer keyboard until it came to me. *What if he was just a bad typist? What if his fingers were off one key?*

"So I tried moving my fingers over one key to the right. Presto, the message came."

Maria looked at the computer screen. "And now you have another message. This one doesn't look like it's the same."

"No, but I think he used the keyboard to make this one too." Willie looked at the screen and then at the keyboard. Then he looked back at the screen.

"The code is made up of numbers and other keyboard marks," Willie said. "The numbers run along the top of the keyboard—"

"And the other marks run along the side!" Maria almost shouted. "Willie, you're a genius."

"I still don't get it," Chris said.

Maria grabbed his arm and dragged him over to the calendar. "What date is the third

Tuesday in July this year?"

Chris reached over and flipped the calendar to July. "It's the 19th. Why?"

"How did you figure that out?" she asked.

"I just ran my eyes across the top to find Tuesday, then ran them down three spaces to the 19th— Oh, now I get it."

Maria and Chris came back to Willie. He was almost done decoding the message. Finally, they all read:

You will find Coco in the old garage down the street.

"The old garage!" Willie shouted. "That's just three blocks away! Let's go!"

"Wait a minute," Maria said. "Shouldn't we wait for the others?" As she spoke, thunder rolled outside the house.

"We can't wait," Willie pleaded. "Coco is waiting for me."

"Willie's right," Chris said. "If you're scared, you can wait here."

"I'm not scared," Maria said. "I'm just not stupid." She watched as the boys headed for the door, then shouted after them, "Wait for me. Someone's got to take care of you two."

It wasn't supposed to be dark for several hours. But thunderclouds hid the sun, and it seemed like dusk. The rain made Maria pause to zip up her coat. Chris was a good runner, but he was having a hard time keeping up with Willie, who had already reached the first corner and was crossing the street to the second block.

By the time they reached the old, closed gas station, the rain had turned into a downpour. Willie reached the large doors just ahead of Chris. Maria got there half a minute later.

"Is this the garage?" Maria asked.

Willie nodded. "That's what everyone calls it." He tugged and tugged on the heavy door. "It's locked," he said. A clap of thunder almost drowned out his voice.

"Let's try the side door," Maria shouted.

Willie followed them around the corner, pushing his wheelchair through the new thick mud. One wheel sank when he pushed as hard as he could. He almost fell out. "Help me, Chris," he shouted. Chris ran back, and together they made it through the mud and onto the sidewalk.

"Over here!" Maria shouted. She held the knob to another door on the side of the building. As Chris and Willie came up to the door, Willie heard something.

"Quiet!" he shouted.

Then they all heard it. Something was scratching from the inside.

Bark!

"Coco! He's in there!" Willie cried.

"The doorknob turns, but the door doesn't open," Maria shouted. Lightning flashed, and Willie saw how wet they were getting.

"Push hard!" Chris said. "Maybe it's just stuck!"

Chris and Maria leaned against the door, and Willie pushed with his hands. The door moved slowly, then pushed open with a *whoosh*. A gray blur of fur leapt from the dark of the doorway into Willie's lap. It was Coco!

"Oh, Coco! I'm so glad to see you!" Willie hugged Coco with all his might. "I'm so sorry, Coco. I promise I'll never hurt you again!"

"See, your prayer did get answered, even if it took a little while," Chris said. "Now, let's get out of this rain and go home."

Lightning split the sky again. Instead of

thunder, however, Willie heard a high-pitched scream.

Willie and Chris turned and looked at Maria. She stood pointing at an old house next door.

"Someone is over there! I saw a man by that house!"

Lightning flashed again, and Willie saw him too. Like a dark shadow, a tall man stood on the dark porch. And he was staring at them.

CHAPTER 10

Secrets Revealed

"Let's get out of here!" Chris yelled. Willie and Maria were way ahead of him. They started moving before he finished the sentence. As fast as the trip down the street had been, they were even faster going back. This time, Maria got there first.

They dashed past Mrs. Shue's and Mrs. Vargas's cars, then burst through the door. Everyone in the room turned and stared as water dripped from them. Mud covered their feet and Willie's wheelchair.

"What a mess!" Grandpa started to shout. Then he saw Coco riding in Willie's lap. "Coco!

You found him!"

Everyone crowded around, laughing and shouting. Coco seemed to enjoy the attention, but he would not leave Willie's lap.

"Well, I guess you two are stuck with each other," Grandpa said. Willie smiled and hugged Coco again.

Chris, Willie, and Maria told the story of the final code and how they solved it. "You should have seen Willie flying down the street," Chris shouted.

"Then I got stuck in the mud," Willie reminded him. But when Willie started to tell about the man on the porch, Chris nudged him, and Maria shook her head.

"Hey, how about coming over tomorrow?" Chris asked when he and Maria finally had to leave.

"Only if I can bring Coco with me," Willie said.

The door closed behind the Vargases, and Grandpa was left with a very muddy Willie and Coco.

"I'm sorry we're such a mess, Grandpa," Willie said. "But it was an emergency."

"I know," Grandpa said. "We just have to get you cleaned up before we go to the airport."

"Airport?" Willie asked. "What for?"

"Have you forgotten what day this is?" Grandpa raised his eyebrow again.

"It's Tuesday the 23rd," Willie said. Then it struck him. "Mom and Dad are coming home!"

Willie took his bath while Grandpa washed Coco. While Willie dried, combed, and dressed, Grandpa wiped off the wheelchair. Finally, they were ready to go.

Willie and Grandpa were quiet most of the way to the airport. Finally, Willie spoke up. "Grandpa, it's raining awfully hard. Can their airplane land all right in this weather?"

"Oh, sure," Grandpa said. "The pilots are all professionals. They've got helpers in the tower to guide them down. And they have radar to see through the clouds."

Willie paused. "But planes do crash, don't they? Especially in bad weather?"

Grandpa patted Willie on the knee. "Willie, you've had lots of experiences in the past few days. What have you learned about prayer and problems like this?"

Willie closed his eyes and thought. "God wants you to ask for what you need. You need to trust Him, even if you don't get what you want or don't get it right away. And, sometimes, God just wants you to talk to Him, even if you can't think of anything you need right then."

Grandpa smiled. "You think God is taking care of your mom and dad up there?"

Willie nodded slowly.

"Then I don't think you need to worry. Let God take care of them."

Willie took a deep breath, rubbed Coco's fur again, and closed his eyes.

Even though Willie agreed with Grandpa, he felt a lot better when Mom and Dad stepped out from the airplane gate. Willie held his arms out wide, and Mom and Dad ran and hugged him together. Coco barked until he got in on the hugging too.

Willie chattered all the way to the car about the codes, Coco's disappearance, and the mysterious person named G.O.D.

"So you still don't have an idea who this G.O.D. person is?" Mom asked finally.

"I have my suspicions," Willie said. "I want to check them out tomorrow."

"If we're lucky, this mystery will keep you busy all summer," chuckled Dad.

"Maybe you should check with George, the mail carrier," Mom said. "He probably knows everyone in town."

"That's it!" Willie said. "Grandpa, stop the car!"

"What?" Grandpa said. "Why?"

"Just stop it, please. Pull in here," Willie said. "I have an idea."

Grandpa turned the car into the town's only ice-cream shop. "I never saw a kid so eager to get an ice cream," he said.

Willie got into his wheelchair and pushed his way into the store. The rain had stopped, and the store was crowded. Willie looked at the people around him, then looked at the flavors. As he was looking, he heard a familiar voice.

"One scoop of rocky road, please."

Then he heard his mom say, "Hello, George, we were just talking about you."

Willie turned his wheelchair and looked up at the man.

"George O. Davis," he said loud enough for everyone in the store to hear. "You're G.O.D.!"

"What?" Mom and Dad said together. Willie looked at Mr. Davis, who was trying to hide his red face behind a rocky-road ice-cream cone.

"Mr. Davis is the mystery person," Willie said with a grin. "It all fits."

"Are you sure?" Grandpa asked.

"Nice Mr. Davis?" Mom asked.

"How could he be?" Dad asked. "He just lives three blocks down the street from us."

Willie looked at his dad, then at Mr. Davis. "You were watching us tonight, weren't you?"

Mr. Davis grinned and nodded. "I was afraid you would hurt yourself over there. So I went to keep an eye on you."

"How did you get my library book?" Willie asked.

"I found it in the bushes by your driveway. It must have dropped out of your car sometime in the past few days."

"Why didn't you just bring Coco back?" Grandpa asked.

"I heard a dog barking this afternoon as I went by the garage, and I thought it was strange. But I didn't know Coco was missing. After I heard that, I was sure that's who it was. I told Willie right away."

Willie nodded. "He did. Right on the computer. How do you know so much about computers? And codes?"

Mr. Davis grinned again. "Computers are

kind of a hobby with me. And I've loved codes since I was your age." He patted Willie's arm. "It drives Mrs. Davis crazy. Stop by some time, and we'll talk her into making cookies."

"That would be great!" Willie said.

Imagine, Willie thought as they headed home, *Mr. George O. Davis is the mystery person.* His head was still whirling when they got home.

"Time for bed, detective," Dad said.

"Just one minute, Dad, OK?" Willie said as he headed for the computer. "I need to check one thing."

Willie switched the computer on and logged into the bulletin board. His hunch had been right. A message waited:

2-12-6 26-9-22 7-12-12 20-12-12-23 26 23-22-7-22-24-7-18-5-22 21-12-9 14-22!

Willie stared at it a long minute before he laughed out loud. "I'm not that backward, Mr. G.O.D." He switched the computer off and went to bed.